First Aid in En

READER

A

What a Fright!

by

ANGUS MACIVER

ISBN 0 7169 5000 6
© *Angus Maciver 1983*

Revised Edition 1998

ROBERT GIBSON · Publisher
17 Fitzroy Place, Glasgow, G3 7SF, Scotland, U.K.

Other books by

ANGUS MACIVER

FIRST AID IN ENGLISH
NEW FIRST AID IN ENGLISH

CONCISE FIRST AID IN ENGLISH
Edited by D.A. MacLennan, M.A.

FIRST AID IN ENGLISH READERS

Reader A — What A Fright!
Reader B — Ali Baba
Reader C — Buried Treasure
Reader D — A Narrow Escape
Reader E — Crossing the Line
Reader F — Kariba

My Book

Name ....

Class ....

School ....

....

....

PREFACE

There is nothing like **Interest** to get children to read well, to read widely, and to understand what they read. **The stories in this book are specially selected to arouse, maintain and satisfy the interest of the pupils**. This interest helps the pupils to overcome many difficulties in the mechanics of diction and to attain an adequate speed of recital.

The Interesting Facts are presented in pictorial form for ease in comprehension at this particular stage. They have a direct bearing on the stories and provide adequate material for expansion of vocabulary and general knowledge.

The Questions on the Stories (Do You Remember ?) are **in sequence** and demand not only that the pupils read carefully but also that they remember the salient points. The answers (oral or written) can be used as **a direct aid to Composition**.

The Development Exercises (Can You Tell ?) endeavour to expand on certain statements in the matter read and the questions are designed to give the pupils an opportunity to **express their thoughts and knowledge, simply and accurately**.

A.M.

ACKNOWLEDGMENTS

We value highly the permission to include copyright material and are happy to put on record our indebtedness for:

Choosing Shoes, by ffrida Wolfe, from "The Very Thing", by permission of the Author's Representatives and Messrs. Sidgwick & Jackson Ltd.

Strange Talk, by Lucy E. Yates, by permission of Messrs. Blackie & Son, Ltd.

The Pig's Tail, by Norman Ault, from "Dreamland Shores", by permission of Oona Ault.

I Wonder, by Jeannie Kirby.

Rufty and Tufty, by Isabell Hempseed, and

Harvest is Coming, by Eunice Fallon, from "The Book of a Thousand Poems", by permission of Messrs. Evans Brothers Ltd.

The Dustman, by Clive Sansom, from "Speech Rhymes", Book I, by permission of the author and Messrs. A. & C. Black Ltd.

The Pencil, by Alethea Chaplin, from "A Treasury of Verse for Little Ones", by permission of Messrs. George G. Harrap & Co. Ltd.

The Doctor, by Rose Fyleman, by permission of the Society of Authors and Miss Rose Fyleman.

My Dog, Spot, by Rodney Bennett, by permission of Joan Bennett.

and for

Mother Hen and Mother Duck, by Eleanor Halsey whom we have been unable to trace.

5

CONTENTS

Contents (continued)

The Greedy Dog

It was a warm day in summer.
A kind butcher gave a bone to a hungry dog.
The animal was happy and wagged his tail.

The dog ran quickly down the street.
He carried the bone in his mouth.
On the way home he had to cross a stream.

The dog looked over the side of the bridge.
In the water he saw another dog.
The other dog had also a bone in his mouth.

He jumped into the water to fight the other dog.
The dog wanted to steal the other bone.
He thought that it was bigger than his own.

The silly creature was nearly drowned.
He opened his mouth and lost his own bone.
It sank to the bottom of the stream.

The greedy dog went home very sad and wet.
Now he had no bone at all.

Do You Remember ?

1. What was the name of the story ?
2. What kind of day was it ?
3. Which season of the year was it ?
4. What did the butcher give to the dog ?
5. How did the dog show that he was happy ?
6. How did the dog carry the bone ?
7. What had he to cross on his way home ?
8. What did the dog see in the water ?
9. What did he do ?
10. What happened to his own bone ?

Can You Tell ?

1. How does a dog show that it is happy ?
2. How does a dog show that it is angry ?
3. What does a dog like to eat ?
4. What should a dog wear round its neck ?
5. Which animals do dogs chase ?
6. Give some pet names of dogs.
7. Name four different kinds of dogs.
8. Which kind of dog do you like best ?
9. Where does your mother buy her meat ?
10. What does a butcher sell ?

Corgi

Spaniel

"Scotty"

"Peke"

Bulldog

Alsatian

Terrier

Exercises

1.   (a) A dog is (a fish, a bird, an animal).
     (b) A dog has (two, four, six) legs.
     (c) A dog has a coat of (hair, wool, feathers).
     (d) A dog (whistles, barks, quacks).
     (e) A dog's foot is called a (paw, hoof, tusk).
     (f) A baby dog is called a (chicken, kitten, puppy).
     (g) A dog's house is called a (stable, kennel, sty).

2. Every sentence should start with a **capital letter** and end with a **full stop**. Write these sentences correctly.
     (a) a butcher gave a bone to a dog
     (b) the dog ran down the street
     (c) the animal had to cross a stream
     (d) in the water he saw another dog
     (e) he wanted to steal the other bone
     (f) the dog jumped into the water
     (g) the silly creature lost his own bone
     (h) it sank to the bottom of the stream

Said Mrs. Hen, "How can you let
Your little children get so wet ?
My little ones are warm and dry
And I should never let them try
To paddle in a muddy brook
Or even at the water look."

Said Mrs. Duck, "But then you see,
My little ducks are just like me,
They like to swim and splash and dive,
Just see how fast they grow and thrive.
But hens will never understand,
That ducks like water not dry land."

Pleasing Everybody

Once a man and his son were going to town.
They wanted to sell their donkey at the market.
They walked and drove the animal in front of
    them.

On the way, a young man spoke to them.
"How foolish you are!" he said.
"The donkey is strong and will carry the boy!"

Soon afterwards, they met a young woman.
"You lazy boy!" she cried.
"Let your poor father ride on the donkey!"

Some time later, an old man spoke to the father.
"You are a very selfish man!" he called.
"There is room on the donkey for the boy!"

Next they met an old woman.
"How cruel you are"! she shouted.
"You should both be carrying the poor donkey!"

The donkey was very heavy to carry.
"How stupid they are!" cried every one.
"Why don't they let the donkey walk ?"

Do You Remember ?

1. What was the name of the story ?
2. Who were going to town ?
3. Why were they going to the market ?
4. What did the young man say to them ?
5. What did the young woman say to the son ?
6. What did the old man say to the father ?
7. What did the old woman say to them ?
8. What did everyone say to them ?
9. Why was it stupid to carry the donkey ?
10. What did they do in the end ?

Can You Tell ?

1. Where do you see donkeys ?
2. What food does a donkey like to eat ?
3. What kind of ears has a donkey ?
4. What pet name do we give to a donkey ?
5. Name animals on which you can ride.
6. On which animal would you like to ride ?
7. Where do you see horses ?
8. Where do you see ponies ?
9. Where can you see elephants and camels ?
10. What kind of person is called a donkey ?

Riding

Young Anansi

A baby son was born to Mr. Anansi, the spider, and his wife and they called him Robin Anansi. The baptism took place on the grass in front of the tree where the Anansis were living.

At midnight in front of the same tree the fairies came to dance. They were friends of Mr. Anansi and his wife. They had gifts for Robin which they laid at the foot of the tree. There were silk sheets, a cradle and some bubble bath.

I am sorry to have to tell you that Robin did not grow up to be a very good spider. Indeed he was a very bad spider. To keep him out of mischief his mother used to sit him on her back when she went to market.

When she wasn't looking he used to make faces at everybody who passed by. He would sometimes stretch out his long front legs and knock ladies' hats off. He never tired of pulling the ears of anyone who had long ears like Mrs. Rabbit and he never tired of pulling the whiskers of anyone who had whiskers like Mr. Cat.

At last his mother promised him that she would give him a good talking to if he did not stop all his pranks. Robin Anansi decided that now he was growing up he would have to behave himself and stop playing tricks on everyone.

The Story of Jumbo

One day a baby elephant was lost in the forest.
Two hunters saw him and caught him with a rope.
They took the young animal to their camp.

The baby elephant followed them everywhere.
He became a pet and was called "Jumbo".
Then the hunters had to return to their own land.

They wanted to take the baby elephant with them.
Jumbo had to travel on a big truck.
He had a keeper who took good care of him.

The young elephant was taken on a very large
  boat.
Poor Jumbo felt very strange on the ship.
He saw nothing but water all around him.

After many days, the boat again reached land.
Jumbo was carried ashore in a big net.
He was afraid of the noise and the tall buildings.

The baby elephant was taken to the animal park.
Jumbo was happy to see grass and trees again.
Many children came to see him at his new home.

Do You Remember ?

1. What was the name of the story ?
2. Who found the baby elephant ?
3. How did they catch him ?
4. Where did they take him ?
5. How did Jumbo leave the camp ?
6. Who looked after the elephant ?
7. How did Jumbo travel across the sea ?
8. How was he carried ashore ?
9. Why was Jumbo afraid ?
10. Where did he go ?

Can You Tell ?

1. Name two fierce wild animals.
2. Name two tame animals.
3. Name two animals which live in water.
4. Name two animals with horns.
5. Name two striped animals.
6. Name two spotted animals.
7. Name two fierce birds.
8. Name two birds which live in water.
9. Name two birds which cannot fly.
10. Name two big crawling creatures.

At the Animal Park

Exercises

1. *(a)* A (horse, squirrel, elephant) has a trunk.
   (b) A (camel, fox, kangaroo) has a hump.
   (c) A (mouse, giraffe, hedgehog) has a long neck.
   (d) A (whale, monkey, pig) is a good climber.
   (e) A (hare, goat, seal) has flippers instead of legs.
   (f) A (rabbit, tiger, donkey) has a fluffy tail.
   (g) A (lion, zebra, sheep) has a coat of wool.

Revision

2. Write correctly:
   (a) a boy ran across the busy road
   (b) his mother told him to be careful
   (c) her name is mary
   (d) peter and john are twins
   (e) we saw him on thursday
   (f) they go to church on sunday
   (g) her birthday is in april
   (h) my holiday starts in july
   (i) he spoke to frank on saturday
   (j) we will meet elsie in september

3. A **singer** is **someone who sings**.
   What name is given to someone who:
   bakes, reads, plays, drives, climbs, skates, hunts, explores, runs, swims?

Robin's Song

Such a litter of leaves on the ground!
Oh! Such a litter!
Not a leaf on the tree to be found,
The wind is so bitter!
And nothing to hear — but the sound,
Of my little twitter!

The fairies have made me a vest,
Velvet and rosy!
Like the glow of the sun in the west,
Or a pretty pink posy!
No wonder I'm singing my best,
So comfy and cosy!

Anonymous

The Fox and the Crow

One day a crow was flying to her nest. She saw a bit of cheese on a window-ledge.

The bird flew down and sat on a fence. She waited until there was no one about. Then she flew with the cheese to a tree.

A hungry fox saw the crow. He wondered how he could get hold of the cheese. Then the animal had a clever idea.

"Hullo, Mrs. Crow!" he called. "How are you?"

The crow just nodded her head.

"How pretty you look!" cried the fox.

The bird was pleased but said nothing.

"You must be a lovely singer!" said the fox.

The foolish bird was so flattered that she tried to sing. As soon as she opened her beak, the cheese fell to the ground.

At once the cunning fox snapped up the cheese and ran off with it.

The stupid crow learned a lesson.

Do You Remember ?

1. What was the name of the story ?
2. Where was the crow going ?
3. What did she see on a window-ledge ?
4. Why did she wait for some time ?
5. Where did the bird go with the cheese ?
6. Who saw the crow ?
7. What did the fox say to her ?
8. What happened when she opened her beak ?
9. What did the cunning fox do ?
10. What lesson did the stupid crow learn ?

Can You Tell ?

1. How does a bird fly ?
2. How does a bird show that it is happy ?
3. How does a bird show that it is angry ?
4. What does a bird like to eat ?
5. Which bird has no nest of her own ?
6. Name several different kinds of birds.
7. Which birds are kept as pets in cages ?
8. Which kind do you like best ? Tell why.
9. Name birds of different colours.
10. Name different places where birds nest.

Birds which fly

Sparrow

Swallow

Parrot

Robin

Eagle

Owl

Pigeon

Blackbird

Seagull

Birds which sometimes fly

Hen

Duck

Turkey

Goose

Swan

Birds which never fly

Emu

Kiwi

Ostrich

Penguin

Exercises

1. (a) A bird has (six, four, two) legs.
    (b) A bird has a coat of (feathers, fur, scales).
    (c) A bird has a (horn, beak, tusk).
    (d) A bird (sings, bleats, neighs).
    (e) A bird has (two, three, four) wings.
    (f) A bird's house is called a (den, hive, nest).
    (g) A baby bird is called a (lamb, nestling, calf).

2. **a, e, i, o, u** are called **vowels**.
    Before a word beginning with **a** or **e** or **i** or **o** or **u**, you must always use **an** instead of **a**.
    Which should be put in each space ?
    (a) My mother was reading __ book.
    (b) His brother ate __ egg.
    (c) My father sat on __ chair.
    (d) The child was just __ infant.
    (e) Jumbo was __ elephant.
    (f) My uncle smokes __ pipe.
    (g) The girl found __ coin.
    (h) The boy wore __ anorak.

3. A **diver** is **a person who dives**.
    What name is given to a person who:
    rides, speaks, jumps, boxes, writes, robs, walks, teaches, drums, talks ?

I Wonder

I wonder why the grass is green,
And why the wind is never seen?

Who taught the birds to build a nest,
And told the trees to take a rest?

Or, when the moon is not quite round,
Where can the missing bit be found?

Who lights the stars, when they blow out,
And makes the lightning flash about?

Who paints the rainbow in the sky,
And hangs the fluffy clouds so high?

Why is it now, do you suppose,
That Dad won't tell me, if he knows?

Jeannie Kirby

The Lion and the Mouse

One day a lion was resting in a forest. Suddenly a mouse ran over his nose. The lion caught the mouse in his big paw.

The little mouse begged for mercy. "Please do not hurt me!" she squeaked.

The lion took pity on her. He opened his paw and let her go free.

"Thank you!" said the mouse. "Some day I will pay back your kindness."

Next morning the mouse heard a great angry roar. She knew that the lion was in trouble. She set off at once to find him.

The mouse saw that her friend was caught in a trap. She nibbled at the net and quickly cut the ropes. In a short time the King of Beasts was free again.

The lion thanked the mouse. "You have saved my life," he said. The lion then ran away to a safe part of the forest.

Do You Remember ?

1. What was the name of the story ?
2. Where was the lion resting ?
3. What did the mouse do to annoy him ?
4. How did the lion catch the mouse ?
5. What did the captured mouse say ?
6. What did the lion do ?
7. What did the mouse hear next morning ?
8. How was the lion caught ?
9. How did the mouse free the lion ?

Can You Tell ?

1. The dog says "_____".
2. The cat says "_____".
3. The sheep says "_____".
4. The cow says "_____".
5. The donkey says "_____".
6. The horse says "_____".
7. The pig says "_____".
8. The duck says "_____".
9. The cock says "_____".
10. The sparrow says "_____".
11. The crow says "_____".
12. The owl says "_____".
13. The hen says "_____".

Exercises

1. bleats, brays, barks, crows, mews, chirps, lows, neighs, chatters, hoots.
   - (a) The dog ___ .   (b) The cat ___ .
   - (c) The sheep ___ . (d) The cow ___ .
   - (e) The cock ___ .   (f) The bird ___ .
   - (g) The owl ___ .   (h) The monkey ___ .
   - (i) The horse ___ .   (j) The donkey ___ .

2. Which should be put in each space — **a** or **an** ?
   - (a) I met ___ boy and ___ girl.
   - (b) ___ train has ___ engine.
   - (c) ___ owl is ___ bird.
   - (d) I have ___ uncle and ___ aunt.
   - (e) ___ monkey is ___ animal.
   - (f) ___ elephant has ___ trunk.
   - (g) He ate ___ apple and ___ orange.
   - (h) ___ acorn grows on ___ oak-tree.
   - (i) The man had ___ axe and ___ saw.
   - (j) I ate ___ egg and ___ slice of toast.

3. Which is **biggest** and which is **smallest** ?
   - (a) lion, mouse, dog, elephant, cat.
   - (b) apple, grape, raisin, lime, melon.
   - (c) sparrow, crow, ostrich, hen, eagle.
   - (d) pail, bath, jug, kettle, cup.

Rufty and Tufty

Rufty and Tufty were two little elves,
Who lived in a hollow oak tree.
They did all the cooking and cleaning
    themselves . . .
And often asked friends in to tea.

Rufty wore blue and Tufty wore red,
And each had a hat with a feather.
Their best Sunday shoes they kept under
    the bed . . .
They were made of magic green leather.

Rufty was clever and kept the accounts,
But Tufty preferred to do cooking.
He could make a fine cake without
    weighing amounts . . .
And eat it when no one was looking.

Isabell Hempseed

Tom was on holiday at the seaside. He loved to play on the sands. One day he was tired and sat on a chair.

Suddenly he saw a ship sailing into the bay. The flag was the Jolly Roger. Tom knew that it was a pirate ship.

Soon after, a small boat came ashore. Three pirates jumped out and quickly caught him. They put him into the boat and went back to the big ship.

Tom was taken before the pirate chief. He looked very fierce and cruel. He gave orders that Tom must walk the plank.

A big plank was put over the side of the ship. They made Tom walk on it. After two steps he fell into the sea.

Splash! Tom woke up in the water. The pirates were all a dream. The tide had come in and upset his chair.

Do You Remember ?

1. What was the name of the story ?
2. Where was Tom on holiday ?
3. Why did he sit on the chair ?
4. What kind of ship did he see ?
5. How many pirates came ashore ?
6. What did they do to Tom ?
7. What kind of man was the pirate chief ?
8. What orders did he give ?
9. Where did Tom wake up ?
10. What had really happened ?

Can You Tell ?

1. Why do people go to the seaside ?
2. Where do you like to go on holiday ?
3. What games can you play ?
4. What kinds of toys do you use ?
5. What kinds of boats do you see ?
6. What birds fly around the shore ?
7. What is a lighthouse ?
8. What is a (1) beach, (2) pier, (3) tide ?
9. What do you enjoy doing on the beach ?
10. Is the sea always the same ?

What A Fright!
At the beach

Exercises

1. *(a)* Why should you be very careful when:
   - (1) wading in the sea? (2) walking on a pier?
   - (3) exploring caves?   (4) sailing in a boat?
   (b) Why should you not go near:
   - (1) big rocks?   (2) steep cliffs?
   - (3) soft quicksands?   (4) living jelly-fish?

Revision

2. *(a)* Write correctly:
   - (1) the boy threw a stone in the water
   - (2) once upon a time there lived a cruel king
   - (3) john and molly are coming on friday
   - (4) both harry and nan were seven in august
   (b) Use **a** or **an**.
   - (1) She gave ___ coin to ___ old beggar.
   - (2) On ___ chair lay ___ empty box.
   - (3) There was ___ knife and ___ fork on the table.
   - (4) We saw ___ eagle and ___ ostrich at the animal park.
3. hat, shoes, ring, scarf, gloves.
   - *(a)* He wore _____ on his feet.
   - *(b)* She wore a _____ round her neck.
   - *(c)* He wore _____ on his hands.
   - *(d)* She wore a _____ on her head.
   - *(e)* She wore a _____ on her finger.

The Pig's Tail

A furry coat has the bear to wear,
The tortoise a coat of mail,
The yak has more than his share of hair,
But — the pig has a curly tail.

The elephant's tusks are sold for gold,
The slug leaves a silver trail,
The parrot is never too old to scold,
But — the pig has a curly tail.

The lion can either roar or snore,
The cow gives milk in a pail,
The dog can guard a door, and more,
But — the pig has a curly tail.

The monkey makes you smile awhile,
The tiger makes you quail,
The fox has many a wile of guile,
But — the pig has a curly tail.

For the rest of the beasts that prey or play,
From the tiny mouse to the whale,
There's much that I could say to-day,
But — the pig has a curly tail.

Norman Ault

Dog Meets Wolf

Dog: Good morning, my friend! How do you do?

Wolf: I am well, thank you! I need not ask how you are! You look the picture of health.

Dog: Yes, I feel fine! I have to work for my living but I have a good kind master. I chase away beggars and frighten any thieves.

Wolf: You certainly look well fed and happy. Look at me! Worry keeps me thin. I have no home as you have. I never know where my next meal is coming from.

Dog: Dear me! What a life! I don't envy you.

Wolf: It is a hard life. I run into danger every day. I could tell you tales that would make your hair stand on end. By the way, what is that ugly mark round your neck?

Dog: It's the mark of my collar. My chain is heavy and makes the collar rub against my neck.

Wolf: A chain! Does your good kind master keep you tied by a chain?

Dog: No . . . not always. I am chained to my kennel at night.

Wolf: I don't envy you now. I like to wander where I please. I would rather be hungry and free than well-fed and chained. Good-bye and good luck, my friend.

Do You Remember ?

1. What was the name of the story ?
2. What did the dog say about his master ?
3. Where did the dog live ?
4. What was his work ?
5. Why was the wolf so thin ?
6. What did the wolf see round the dog's neck ?
7. What caused the mark ?
8. When was the dog chained ?
9. To what was he tied ?
10. What would the wolf rather be ?

Can You Tell ?

1. Which kind of dog is:
   (a) rounding up sheep ?
   (b) pulling the sledge ?
   (c) checking luggage ?
   (d) searching for someone lost in the snow ?
   (e) guiding the blind person ?
   (f) catching the thief ?
2. Describe what you see in each of the pictures.
3. In the story, which animal do you think was the luckier ? Why ?

Working Dogs

Sheep dog

Sledge dog

Sniffer dog

Rescue dog

Guide dog

Police dog

Exercises

1. fruit, bird, flower, animal, insect, vegetable, fish, tree.

   (a) Wolf is the name of an ____.
   (b) Sparrow is the name of a ____.
   (c) Daisy is the name of a ____.
   (d) Plum is the name of a ____.
   (e) Carrot is the name of a ____.
   (f) Oak is the name of a ____.
   (g) Fly is the name of an ____.
   (h) Shark is the name of a ____.

2. **Singular** means **a single one**.
   Plural means **more than one**.

   We say one **book** but say two **books**.

   (a) We say one **toy** but say ten ____.
   (b) We say one **desk** but say six ____.
   (c) We say one **brush** but say four ____.
   (d) We say one **class** but say five ____.
   (e) We say one **leaf** but say many ____.
   (f) We say one **shelf** but say two ____.
   (g) We say one **knife** but say three ____.
   (h) We say one **wife** but say many ____.

3. With what are you able to:

   see, smell, hear, feel, taste?

Comfort

The wind is blowing cold outside,
And calling to come in,
But I am cuddled up in bed,
With blankets to my chin.
A bottle hot is at my feet,
My arms are tucked in tight,
Call as you will, oh Mr. Wind!
You can't come in tonight!

The window panes are rattling hard,
As loud the east wind blows,
But I am cuddled up in bed,
With blankets to my nose.
My little bed is soft and warm,
And I have blankets three,
Blow as you will, oh Mr. Wind!
You can't come in to me!

Anonymous

An Honest Man

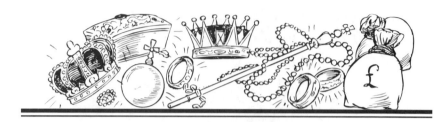

A king, who once ruled in a far-away land, was very worried, His trusted old servant had died, and a new watchman was needed to guard the royal treasure.

"I must be very careful," he said to himself. "I must not choose a thief, because he would rob me. I wonder how I can find an honest man for the job?"

He sent for his chief lord, who was very wise and clever. "My friend," said the king. "I need a watchman to guard the royal treasure. I want you to find the most honest man in my kingdom."

"That will be very difficult," replied the chief lord. "I will come back again tomorrow and tell you what to do."

Next day the chief lord returned to the palace. "Here is my plan," he said to the king. "Prepare a feast and invite to it everyone who would like to be your watchman."

The king prepared a great feast and invited all those who wished to guard his treasure. As each man arrived at the palace, he was told how to reach the feasting hall. On the way he had to walk alone through a long passage. On each side of the passage were large sacks which were full of gold and silver coins.

When the feast was over, the chief lord spoke to the men. "I hope you have enjoyed the food. The king now wishes you to dance."

Strange to say, nobody moved. They all began to make excuses . . . all except

one man. This man came forward and danced a jig up and down the hall.

"That is the honest man," said the chief lord to the king. "All the others have taken some gold and silver from the sacks. They are afraid to dance because the coins would jingle and fall out of their pockets. That man did not touch the money and so he is not afraid to dance."

The king was very pleased. He rewarded the chief lord for his cleverness, and the honest man was made watchman over the treasure.

Do You Remember ?

1. What was the name of the story ?
2. Why was the king very worried ?
3. For whom did he send ?
4. What did the king ask the chief lord to do ?
5. What did the chief lord tell the king to do ?
6. What happened when the men reached the palace ?
7. What was on each side of the passage ?
8. What did the chief lord ask the men to do ?
9. Why were all, except one, afraid to dance ?
10. How did the king show that he was pleased ?

Can You Tell ?

1. Who stays in a royal palace ?
2. Where do you often see a cottage ?
3. Why is the Arab tent low and flat ?
4. What is a skyscraper ?
5. Who lived in tepees and wigwams ?
6. (a) In winter the Eskimo lived in an ____.
   (b) What is an igloo made of ?
7. Would you like to live in a caravan ? Tell why.
8. What is a log-cabin made of ?

Homes

Palace

Cottage

Arab tent

Skyscraper

Igloo

Thatched hut

Caravan

Log cabin

Exercises

1. nest, stable, sty, kennel, hive, coop, fold, byre, burrow, den.
   (a) A bee lives in a ——— .
   (b) A bird lives in a ——— .
   (c) A dog lives in a ——— .
   (d) A pig lives in a ——— .
   (e) A horse lives in a ——— .
   (f) A cow lives in a ——— .
   (g) A rabbit lives in a ——— .
   (h) A hen lives in a ——— .
   (i) A lion lives in a ——— .
   (j) A sheep lives in a ——— .

2. **Singular . . . Plural**
   We say one **fork** but say two **forks**.
   (a) We say one **baby** but say four ——— .
   (b) We say one **fairy** but say many ——— .
   (c) We say one **dish** but say many ——— .
   (d) We say one **monkey** but say four ——— .
   (e) We say one **man** but say five ——— .
   (f) We say one **mouse** but say many ——— .
   (g) We say one **sheep** and say six ——— .
   (h) We say one **deer** and say many ——— .

3. Put **a** or **an** in the spaces
   (a) He had — stamp and — envelope.
   (b) They played — organ and — piano.
   (c) We saw — ox and — ass.

Mister Nobody

I know a funny little man,
As quiet as a mouse,
Who does the mischief that is done,
In everybody's house!

There's no one ever sees his face,
And yet we all agree,
That every plate we break was cracked
By Mr. Nobody.

'Tis he who always tears our books,
And leaves the door ajar,
He pulls the buttons from our coats,
And scatters pins afar.

The ink we never spill; the shoes
That lying around you see,
Are not **our** shoes: they all belong
To Mr. Nobody.

Anonymous

Only Pretending

Peter and Mary were brother and sister. One bright summer day they went for a walk in the woods near their home. All at once they came upon a strange furry animal about the size of a rabbit. It was scratching insects out of an old tree-stump and gobbling them up.

When the animal turned and saw them, a queer thing happened. It seemed to drop dead on the ground.

"Oh! What a pity!" cried Mary. "We've given it such a fright that we've killed it!"

The animal certainly looked dead. It lay on its side and was perfectly still.

"I do not know what kind of animal it is," said Peter. "It has a nice smooth fur coat. Let's take it home to father and he will tell us what it is!"

"Be careful!" warned Mary. "It may scratch you if you touch it!"

"Not if it's dead!" replied Peter.

The animal was perfectly still while Peter picked it up. The boy held it stretched across his arms and looked at it closely.

The animal did not move.

"It's dead!" said Peter.

The boy carried the animal while his sister ran ahead to tell their father. When Mary arrived at the house, she went inside to look for him.

Mary was away for such a long time that Peter wondered what was the matter. He laid the animal on the bottom step, and walked towards the door. Just as he reached it, he met his father and sister.

Peter turned and pointed to the bottom step. "Look! There's our strange animal!"

Peter blinked in surprise. The animal was gone, and the step was bare.

Suddenly Mary shouted, "There it is!" They saw the animal dart across the garden and disappear into the bushes.

Their father laughed loudly. "You have been tricked," he said. "That sly little animal is called an opossum. It can lie perfectly still for a long time and look as if it were dead. Then, when it gets a good chance of escape, it runs away."

"What a clever animal!" cried Mary.

"Yes," replied her father. "The opossum was only pretending."

Do You Remember ?

1. What was the name of the story ?
2. What was the boy's name ?
3. What was the girl's name ?
4. What was the strange animal doing in the woods ?
5. About what size was the animal ?
6. What did the animal do when it saw them ?
7. Where did Peter carry it ?
8. Where did he leave it ?
9. Who came to see what it was ?
10. Why did Peter blink in surprise ?
11. Where did the animal go ?
12. What kind of animal was it ?

Can You Tell ?

Which creature has a covering of:

     (a) wool ?   (b) fur ?
     (c) hair ?   (d) feathers ?
     (e) scales ?   (f) thick skin ?
     (g) shell ?   (h) spines ?

Coverings

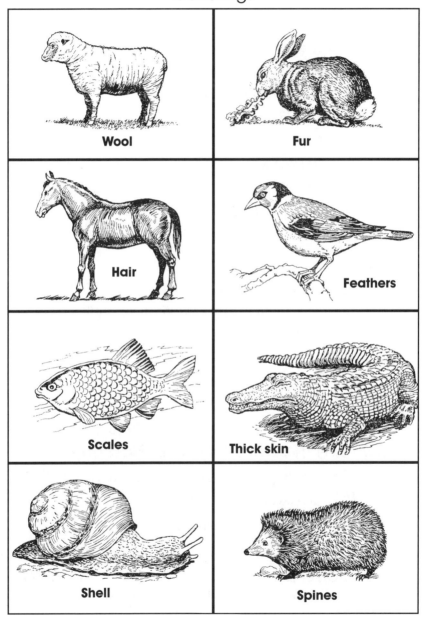

Wool	**Fur**
Hair	**Feathers**
Scales	**Thick skin**
Shell	**Spines**

Exercises

1. hair, wool, fur, thick skin, spines, scales, feathers, shell.

   (a) A lamb has a coat of _____ .

   (b) A parrot has a coat of _____ .

   (c) A fox has a coat of _____ .

   (d) A tortoise has a coat of _____ .

   (e) A herring has a coat of _____ .

   (f) A porcupine has a coat of _____ .

   (g) A camel has a coat of _____ .

   (h) An elephant has a coat of _____ .

2. *(a)* Write correctly:

   (1) we met david and nancy on tuesday

   (2) last saturday was the first day of october

   (b) Use **a** or **an**.

   (1) The hunter had __ bow and __ arrow.

   (2) She wore __ cap and __ apron.

   (3) The man hurt __ arm and __ leg.

   (c) Give the word for **more than one**

   (1) chair,   (2) box,   (3) loaf,   (4) story,   (5) donkey,   (6) foot.

3. We often see the **two together.**

   (a) cup and s _ _ _ _ r.   *(b)* knife and f _ _ k.

   (c) bread and b _ _ _ _ r. *(d)* ham and e _ g.

   (e) pepper and s _ _ t.   *(f)* sugar and m _ _ k.

The wind sang to the cornfields
A happy little song,
And this is what he whispered,
"The harvest won't be long."

The wind sang to the windmill
A merry little tune.
The windmill answered gaily,
"The harvest's coming soon."

The whispering of the poppies
Through the cornfields steals along,
They are joining with the fairies
Singing harvest's merry song.

Eunice Fallon. Poem "August"

One day Tom and his young sister Jane went to shop in the village. As they walked along the road, Tom saw a horseshoe lying on the ground.

"Look, Jane!" he cried. "A horseshoe! Pick it up and keep it for luck!"

"I will not!" replied Jane. "A horseshoe is of no use to me!"

Without saying anything, Tom picked up the horseshoe and carried it in his hand.

When they reached the village, Tom went to see the blacksmith. He sold the horseshoe to him for several coins. Afterwards they visited the grocer's shop, the butcher's shop, and the baker's shop. There they bought all the things they had been told to get.

Suddenly Tom left Jane and dashed across the street. He entered the little shop which sold fruit and sweets. When he came out he was carrying something in a brown paper bag.

They did not stay long in the village as they wanted to be home in time for dinner. On the way, Jane became very tired and thirsty. Although Tom carried the heavy basket, she could not keep up with him. Poor Jane walked slowly along the road some distance behind her brother.

Suddenly she saw a lovely ripe cherry lying on the road. Jane bent down and picked it up. After cleaning it with her handkerchief, she put it into her mouth. Oh, how nice and fresh it tasted!

Jane had not gone very far when she found a second cherry. She picked it up, cleaned it, and ate it. A little later she found a third cherry. Jane did the same as before. She picked it up, cleaned it, and ate it. In this way, she picked up a dozen cherries, one after the other.

When they reached the gate, Tom stopped and waited for his sister. "Jane!" he said. "You don't know it, but I have played a trick on you. Those cherries, which you picked up, were mine. I paid for them with the money I got for the horseshoe. I made a hole in the side of the bag so that the cherries would fall out. Now, if you had bent once only to pick up the horseshoe, you would not have bent twelve times for the cherries."

Do You Remember ?

 1. What was the name of the story ?
 2. Where were Tom and his sister going ?
 3. What did Tom see on the road ?
 4. What did he tell his sister to do ?
 5. What did she reply ?
 6. To whom did Tom sell the horseshoe ?
 7. Which shops did they visit ?
 8. In the story, Jane was _____ and _____ .
 9. What did she see lying on the road ?
10. What did she do ?
11. How many cherries did she eat ?
12. Tell how Tom tricked his young sister.

Can You Tell ?

 1. How does a horse show that it is happy ?
 2. How does a horse show that it is angry ?
 3. What does a horse like to eat ?
 4. Why does a horse wear iron shoes ?
 5. How is a horse guided ?
 6. What name is given to the long hair on a horse's neck ?
 7. What is a saddle ?
 8. What has taken the place of the horse on the farm ?
 9. Who do we see riding a horse in town ?
10. Which way should a horseshoe be hung on a door or wall ? Explain why.

The Horse

Chariot

Stage coach

Horse and cart

Horse and plough

Knight on horseback

Arab

Jockey

Huntsman

Collar

Life-guard

Saddle

Exercises

1. *(a)* A horse is (a bird, a fish, an animal).
   (b) A horse has (two, four, six) legs.
   (c) A horse has a coat of (hair, wool, feathers).
   (d) A horse (quacks, mews, neighs).
   (e) A horse's foot is called a (paw, hoof, horn).
   (f) A baby horse is called a (foal, cub, calf).
   (g) A horse's house is called a (barn, sty, stable).

2. The proper names of **persons** and **places** should always start with a **capital letter**.
   Write correctly:
   (a) tom brown, connie jones, richard miller, lily taylor.
   (b) mr. smart, mrs. cook, miss clark, master young.
   (c) queen elizabeth, prince charles, princess anne.
   (d) manchester, glasgow, cardiff, belfast.
   (e) wales, ireland, england, scotland.

3. Give words **opposite** in meaning to: up, big, bad, top, sad, wide, thick, cruel, lost, buy.

4. We often see the **two together**.
   (a) bat and b _ _ l.
   (b) needle and t _ _ _ _ d.
   (c) brush and c _ _ b.
   (d) pen and i _ k.
   (e) lock and k _ y.

Strange — Is It Not ?

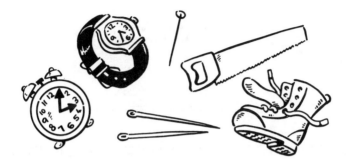

A pin has a head but has no hair,
A clock has a face, but no mouth there,
Needles have eyes but they cannot see,
A hill has a foot, but has no knee,
A watch has hands, but has no fingers,
Boots have tongues, but are not singers,
Rivers run, though they have no feet,
And a saw has teeth, but it cannot eat.

Anonymous

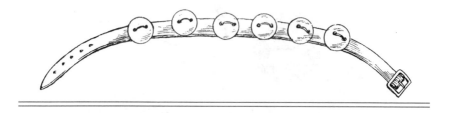

Once upon a time some mice lived in the house of an old man. They ran across the floors and climbed into cup-boards in search of crumbs of bread and bits of cheese. No one bothered them as they scampered in and out of their holes. Then, one day, a large grey tabby cat came to live in the house.

To the mice, this cat was a great grey monster with big shining eyes and strange bad habits. Not only did she try to catch them but she used to clean herself three or four times a day. She did this by licking herself with her tongue.

The mice began to get worried. No longer could they do as they pleased. If they crept out to look for food, the cat chased them back at once. They would starve if she stayed in the house much longer. Something would have to be done!

The mice made up their minds that they must get rid of the cat. They held a meeting but instead of making plans they just kept on complaining.

Then a young mouse stepped forward. "Listen! I have a good idea. My plan won't get rid of the cat, but we will be safe."

"Tell us about it!" squealed the other mice.

The young mouse spoke again. "The wicked cruel cat walks about so quietly that we cannot hear her. Let us fasten a bell round her neck. When she walks, the bell will ring and warn us of danger."

"That's a splendid idea!" cried some mice. "Put a bell round the cat's neck and then we will all be safe."

Suddenly a wise old mouse spoke. "It would be a clever plan but for one thing. Who is going to fasten the bell round the cat's neck?"

The old mouse turned to the young mouse "It is your plan. Will you tie the bell on the cat?"

"No-no! I am not feeling very well," replied the young mouse.

The wise old mouse spoke again. "Remember! It is one thing to make a plan and another thing to carry it out. If no one will put a bell on the cat, then we must do as we have always done. As soon as you see the cat, run as fast as you can and try to escape."

Do You Remember ?

1. What was the name of the story ?
2. Who ran about as they pleased in the old man's house ?
3. Where did they search for food ?
4. Who came to live there ?
5. What very bad habits had she ?
6. How did she clean herself ?
7. Why did the mice begin to get worried ?
8. What did they make up their minds to do ?
9. What was the young mouse's plan ?
10. What did the wise old mouse ask ?
11. Why would the plan not work ?
12. What did the wise old mouse tell them to do ?

Can You Tell ?

1. Why should you keep yourself clean and tidy ?
2. How do the following wash themselves:
   people, birds, cats, elephants ?
3. What is the proper way to clean your:
   hair, skin, teeth, fingernails, clothes, shoes ?
4. Why is soap and hot water best for washing ?
5. Name any creatures which don't have to wash because they live in water.

Washing and Cleaning

Exercises

1. bell, brush, pan, match, pencil, needle, book, soap, chair, ladder.

   Which of them are used in:
   sweeping, writing, sitting, ringing, washing, climbing, lighting, reading, cooking, sewing?

2. (a) Ice is **cold** but fire is ____ .
   (b) Soot is **black** but snow is ____ .
   (c) A hare is **fast** but a snail is ____ .
   (d) A giant is **tall** but a dwarf is ____ .
   (e) The sun shines by **day** but the moon shines by ____ .
   (f) A door will **open** or ____ .
   (g) A tap can be turned **off** or ____ .
   (h) A sum is **correct** or ____ .
   (i) A knife may be **blunt** or ____ .
   (j) A puzzle may be **easy** or ____ .

3. Put **I** or **me** in the spaces.

   (a) ___ want to read the book.
   (b) He asked ___ about the pencil.
   (c) ___ fell on the floor.
   (d) Do you wish ___ to go ?
   (e) My mother gave it to ___ .
   (f) ___ am waiting for my sister.

Twinkle, Twinkle, Little Star

Twinkle, twinkle, little star,
How I wonder what you are,
Up above the world so high,
Like a diamond in the sky.

When the blazing sun is set,
When the grass with dew is wet,
Then you show your little light,
Twinkle, twinkle, all the night.

In the dark blue sky you keep,
And often through my window peep,
For you never shut your eye,
Till the sun is in the sky.

And your bright and tiny spark
Lights the traveller in the dark.
Though I know not what you are,
Twinkle, twinkle, little star.

Jane Taylor

The Miser's Gold

Once upon a time there was a selfish old man. He lived all by himself in a little cottage. Now this old man had a big bag of gold. Every night he would take out his gold and count it.

"I am a rich man," he said to himself, "All this gold belongs to me. I will keep it in the chest. No one will ever get a share of it."

One dark night a robber was passing the old man's house. He saw the light and looked through the window. At that moment the old miser was hiding his gold.

"Ah!" said the robber. "I will wait until the old man has gone to bed. Then I will steal his money."

Later that night the robber crept quietly into the house. The old miser was fast asleep and did not hear him. The robber stole the bag of gold and ran away.

Now there was a little hole in the bottom of the bag. One by one, the gold coins fell out. Soon the bag was empty.

The robber was very, very angry. He had lost all the gold. He could not find the money because it was dark.

"I will sleep here in the forest," he said to himself. "I will rise early in the morning. It will be easy to find the gold in daylight."

At dawn next morning a strange thing happened. Who came dancing along the forest path but a fairy! She saw all the gold coins scattered on the grass.

"Oh!" she cried. "Some one has stolen the old miser's gold. What shall I do? If I give it back to him, he will only hide it again. He is such a mean and greedy man."

The fairy touched the gold coins with her magic wand. At once they changed into lovely golden daffodils.

"That is much better," she said, "These flowers will make children happy."

Suddenly the fairy saw the sleeping robber. "This bad man must be punished." said the fairy. "He should not take what is not his own."

She touched the robber with her magic wand. The robber awoke and tried to speak. Instead he made a horrid croaking sound. When he tried to run away, he found himself hopping about from place to place.

The fairy had changed him into an ugly old toad.

Do You Remember ?

1. What was the name of the story ?
2. Where did the old man live ?
3. What did he do every night ?
4. Who happened to pass the cottage ?
5. What did he see through the window ?
6. What did the robber do ?
7. What caused the gold to fall out of the bag ?
8. Why could he not find the lost money ?
9. Where did the robber sleep that night ?
10. When did the fairy visit the forest ?
11. What did she do to the gold coins ?
12. What did she do to the sleeping robber ?

Can You Tell ?

1. What is a garden ?
2. Name three garden flowers.
3. Name three wild flowers.
4. Do you have any of these flowers in your house ?
5. How do you give flowers a drink in dry weather ?
6. Which flower do you like best ? Tell why.
7. What is the name of a man who works in a garden ?
8. What tools does a gardener use ?
9. What kind of shop sells flowers ?
10. Which insect flies from flower to flower ? Tell why.

Wild Flowers

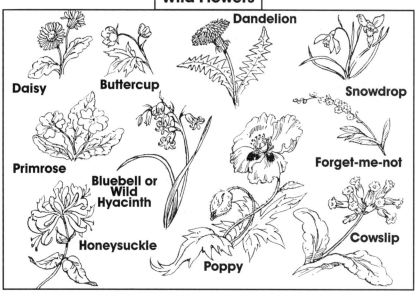

Dandelion

Daisy

Buttercup

Snowdrop

Primrose

Forget-me-not

Bluebell or
Wild
Hyacinth

Honeysuckle

Poppy

Cowslip

Garden Flowers

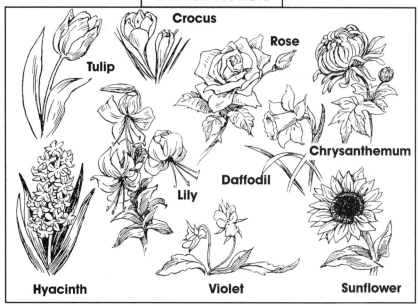

Crocus

Rose

Tulip

Chrysanthemum

Daffodil

Lily

Hyacinth

Violet

Sunflower

Exercises

1. rose, daisy, heather, grass, buttercup.
   - (a) as green as the ____ .
   - (b) as white as a ____ .
   - (c) as yellow as a ____ .
   - (d) as red as a ____ .
   - (e) as purple as the ____ .

2. Write correctly:
   - (a) i met mr. smith on thursday
   - (b) new york is a great city in america
   - (c) we will visit london at easter

3. Give **plural** of:
   - (a) cup,   (b) table,   (c) boy,   (d) poppy,
   - (e) wolf,   (f) tooth.

4. Give **opposites** of:
   - (a) Tom was **rude** but Fred was ____ .
   - (b) Summer is **hot** but winter is ____ .
   - (c) A stone **sinks** but a cork ____ .

5. Put **I** or **me** in the spaces.
   - (a) ___ bought some sweets.
   - (b) She pushed ___ .
   - (c) Give ___ that paper.
   - (d) In the garden ___ saw a bird.

The Pencil

I'm just a little pencil
That's made of wood and lead;
My head is long and pointed,
My body smooth and red.
I once was long and handsome,
But now I soon must die;
I like to write quite nicely,
But master does not try.
He treats me very badly,
And often shaves my head,
He cuts me so unkindly,
That I shall soon be dead.
He sucks me too — I hate it —
And puts me in the ink —
Have I not cause to grumble?
Just tell me what you think.

Alethea Chaplin

The Three Wishes

Once there was a woodcutter who lived with his wife in a hut near a forest. One day he sharpened his axe and set out to cut down some branches for his winter firewood.

As he entered the forest he heard a sudden call for help. The woodman rushed to the rescue and quickly reached the spot. He found a tiny old man caught among the thorn bushes. The woodcutter cut away some branches with his axe and set him free.

In return for his kindness, the tiny little man said, "I know that you are poor, and I want to help you. I will give you three wishes. Wish anything that you please and you shall have it."

Without waiting to cut his firewood, the woodcutter hurried home. When he reached the hut, he told the good news to his wife.

"Oh, how wonderful!" she said. "Let us sit down and think of the lovely things we can have with our wishes."

"I am very hungry," said the woodcutter. "We can talk about our good luck while we eat."

As soon as the dinner was ready, they sat at the table and began to eat and talk.

"We can wish for plenty of money," said the woodcutter.

"We can ask for a house like a palace," said his wife.

"We can wish to be king and queen," said the husband.

"We can wish for rich clothes and jewels," said his wife.

They could not make up their minds what to ask for first. Then the man said, "This dinner is not very good. I wish I had a nice big sausage to eat with this bread."

As soon as he spoke, a large sausage appeared on the table.

His wife was very angry and kept scolding him. "You silly man! You have wasted one of the wishes! How could you be so stupid? Oh! I wish the sausage was sticking to your nose!"

As soon as she said these words, the sausage jumped up and stuck to his nose. In vain they tried to pull it off.

It was the man's turn to be angry. "You silly woman!" he cried. "Why did you make such a wish? I cannot go about with a sausage hanging to my nose! I wish the sausage would go back to the table."

The sausage suddenly dropped to the table. The woodcutter and his wife looked sadly at each other. The three wishes were gone and they were still as poor as ever.

Do You Remember ?

1. What was the name of the story?
2. Who lived in a hut hear a forest?
3. Why did the woodcutter go out with his axe?
4. Who was caught among the thorn bushes?
5. What did the little man say when he was free?
6. To whom did the woodcutter tell the good news?
7. What did they talk about at dinner?
8. Why did the sausage appear on the table?
9. What did his wife say?
10. What happened next?
11. What did the woodcutter say?
12. Why did they look sadly at each other?

Can You Tell ?

Who uses at his work:

(a) a saw?   (b) an anvil?
(c) a brush?   (d) a pair of shears?
(e) weighing scales?   (f) a pair of scissors?
(g) a chopper?   (h) an axe?
(i) a safety lamp?   (j) a flat trowel?

Working Tools

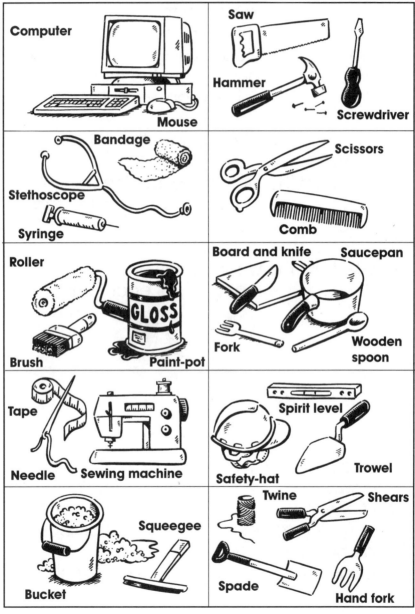

Computer

Mouse

Saw

Hammer

Screwdriver

Bandage

Stethoscope

Syringe

Scissors

Comb

Roller

GLOSS

Brush

Paint-pot

Board and knife

Saucepan

Fork

Wooden spoon

Tape

Needle

Sewing machine

Spirit level

Safety-hat

Trowel

Squeegee

Bucket

Twine

Shears

Spade

Hand fork

Exercises

1. spade, axe, knife, hammer, saw, sponge, key, brush.
    (a) He cut the bread with a ____ .
    (b) He locked the door with a ____ .
    (c) He dug the garden with a ____ .
    (d) He hit nail with a ____ .
    (e) He washed the car with a ____ .
    (f) He chopped down the tree with an ____ .
    (g) He painted the walls with a ____ .
    (h) He cut through the plank with a ____ .

2. A **noun** is the **name** of anything.
    Pick out the **name words**.
    (a) Cows eat grass.
    (b) The girl wrote a letter.
    (c) The child dropped the doll on the floor.
    (d) After supper, the children went to bed.
    (e) The parcel came from Paris in France.
    (f) Hens lay eggs.
    (g) A boy kicked the ball.
    (h) The man lit his pipe with a match.
    (i) Near the cave, the hunters saw a fire.
    (j) Next Sunday will be the last day of April.

3. What colours are they ?
    sugar, blood, soot, butter, sky, tar, milk, moon.

The Dustman

Every Thursday morning
Before we're quite awake,
Without the slightest warning
The house begins to shake
With a Biff! Bang!
Biff! Bang! Biff!
It's the dustman who begins
Bang! Crash!
To empty all the bins
Of their rubbish and their ash
With a Biff! Bang!
Biff! Bang! Crash!

Clive Sansom

A New Way to Fish

One very cold day in winter a large brown bear met a sly fox. The fox was carrying a big string of fish which he had stolen.

"My goodness!" said the bear. "What a lovely catch! I am very fond of fish. Where did you get them?"

"I caught them in the river," replied the fox. "Where did you think I got them? They don't grow on trees."

"I know that," growled the bear. "I have been fishing for years but never caught so many. I thought I knew all the best places around here."

"If I tell you, will you keep it a secret?" asked the fox.

"Of course I will!" replied the bear. "You can trust me."

"I have a new way of fishing," said the fox. "I don't try to catch fish with my paws as you do. I use my brains and I always get as many as I want."

"How do you do it?" asked the bear.

"If you want a big catch," said the fox, "here is what you must do. Go down to the river late at night and make a hole in the ice. Stick your tail down into the water and keep it there as long as you can. When the fish bite, you must not mind if your tail hurts a little. At sunrise, pull up your tail and you'll find dozens of fish hanging on to it."

That very night, the bear did as the fox

had told him. He made a hole in the ice and stuck his tail down into the water.

The more his tail hurt, the more fish he thought he had caught.

When morning came, the bear gave his tail a pull. Nothing happened. He gave another pull. His tail did not move. In a rage he gave a very hard pull. There was a loud crack and he was free.

The bear turned round to see how many fish he had caught. Not a fish was to be seen! Instead he saw a part of his tail still stuck in the ice.

The bear knew then that the fox had played a trick on him. He looked at his tail. Instead of a nice long one he had now a short stumpy one. The fox was very lucky that he did not meet the bear again for a long, long time.

Do You Remember ?

1. What was the name of the story?
2. Who met each other?
3. What kind of day was it?
4. What was the fox carrying?
5. Where did the fox say that he caught them?
6. How did the bear catch fish?
7. What new way had the fox?
8. When did the bear go to fish?
9. What did he do?
10. When did he pull up his tail?
11. What happened to it?
12. Why was the fox lucky?

Can You Tell ?

1. Name as many kinds of fish as you can.
2. Which kinds are big and which are small?
3. Give different ways of catching fish.
4. Which kind of fish do you like best?
5. Name an animal which likes to eat fish?
6. Why is the whale **not** a fish?
7. What is the name of the largest fish?

Fishing

Exercises

1. *(a)* A fish lives (in the air, on land, in the water).
   (b) A fish (walks, swims, flies).
   (c) A fish has (fins, arms, legs).
   (d) A fish has a coat of (wool, scales, feathers).
   (e) A fish has (big eyes, small eyes, no eyes).

2. Pick out the **nouns**.
   (a) Mice like cheese.
   (b) The lady bought a hat.
   (c) The dog chased a cat down the road.
   (d) In the morning the ducks swam across the river.
   (e) On Friday the Queen returned to London.

3. We use **is** when we are speaking of **one**.
   We use **are** when we are speaking of **more than one**. Put **is** or **are** in the spaces.
   (a) My plate __ empty
   (b) The kittens __ young.
   (c) Your shoes __ wet.
   (d) His knife __ sharp.
   (e) He __ angry.
   (f) We __ sorry.

4. Give the words **opposite in meaning** to —
   (a) empty,   *(b)* young,
   (c) wet,   *(d)* sharp,
   (e) high.

The Rainbow Fairies

Two little clouds, one summer day,
Went flying through the sky;
They went so fast they bumped their heads,
And both began to cry.

Old Father Sun looked down and said:
"Oh, never mind my dears,
I'll send my little fairy folk
To dry your falling tears."

One fairy came in violet,
And one wore indigo;
In blue, green, yellow, orange, red,
They made a pretty row.

They wiped the cloud-tears all away,
And then from out the sky,
Upon a line the sunbeams made,
They hung their gowns to dry.

Anonymous

The Frog and the Ox

One day, an ox was walking through the marshy ground near a pond, when it tramped among a number of young frogs. Some of the frogs were kicked to death, some were squeezed underfoot and made to sink into the mud. Only a few escaped unhurt.

One of the lucky ones who had managed to miss the blows, hopped off very quickly to its mother. She was rather a big frog and very proud of her

size. As they sat together on the grass in the park, she was very annoyed to hear of this huge animal. "What kind of thing was it? And how big was it?" she asked. And you could easily tell she was excited by the way she asked two questions at once. She blew herself out. "Was it bigger than this?" she asked. "Bigger than you?" said her son. "Why, mother, even if you were to blow yourself up and up till you burst, you would not be nearly so big as that animal." Mrs. Frog was very hurt at this. Just to show him, she would have one more puff, she thought. She did. And she burst.

Aesop Fable (Adapted)

Do You Remember ?

1. What happened to the frogs when the ox stepped among them?
2. To whom did one of the frogs go at once?
3. How could you tell that mother frog was excited?
4. How did her son warn her?

Can You Tell ?

1. Why was the mother frog angry?
2. What might she have been thinking about, instead of being angry?
3. Did she take the warning which her son gave her?
4. How do you know?
5. Which of the following describe Mrs. Frog: proud, big, selfish?
6. Which of the following interested her more: her own importance, the safety of her family?
7. Was she a good mother?

Interesting Facts about Frogs

Frogs eggs beginning to hatch into tadpoles

Tadpoles 4 weeks old: the feathers are gills

Three weeks from tadpole to frog

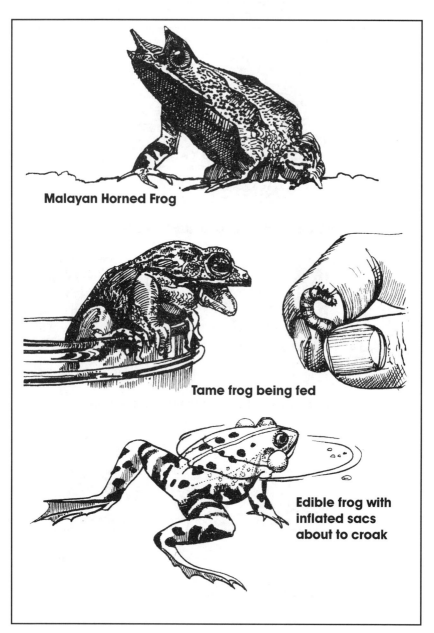

Malayan Horned Frog

Tame frog being fed

Edible frog with inflated sacs about to croak

The Sun and the Wind

One day the Sun and the Wind were arguing about which was the stronger. They could not agree about it. At that very moment, they saw a man walking along a road on the earth down below. They made up their minds that each would try to make him stop walking. The Wind tried first. It blew loud and strong, but the man simply pulled his coat close to him, drew on his hat and walked on. Louder and stronger blew the Wind, but still the man did not stop. Then the Wind drew in its breath for one last, mighty blow. But the man simply tightened his belt, grasped his coat firmly and then, with his head bent forward, he forced his way along.

Then came the Sun's turn. First it removed the dull clouds that the storm had caused. Then it smiled down on the earth below and the land felt the gentle heat. Then the Sun smiled more and more, and it shone more brightly than ever. Soon the man had to take off his coat and then his hat. Then he began to wave his hat to and fro like a fan. The Sun smiled more broadly than ever and, in the end, the man had to stop and take shelter under a big, leafy tree. It was a proud Sun that set that night, for the great and strong Wind had to admit that the Sun had beaten him.

Aesop Fable (Adapted)

Do You Remember ?

1. What were the Sun and the Wind arguing about?
2. Who tried first?
3. What did the Wind do?
4. What did the man do?
5. What did the Wind do next?
6. What did the Sun do first?
7. How did the earth know what the Sun was doing?
8. What did it do next?
9. What did the Sun do after that?
10. What did the man do then?
11. What did he do after that?
12. What had the man to do in the end?

Can You Tell ?

1. Did the Sun or the Wind make the man do what it wanted?
2. Who won — the Wind or the man?
3. Who won — the Sun or the man?
4. Who was the stronger — Sun or Wind?
5. Which one tried to get its own way with noise and bullying?
6. Which one tried to get its own way gently and quietly and pleasantly?
7. Which is the better way?
8. The sun shines or beams. Give two words each for what the following do: rain, thunder, stars.
9. Use your dictionary to find the meanings of:
    hurricane, typhoon, breeze, tornado.
10. Find another name for:
    stop, shelter, land, storm.

The Doctor

He comes with mother up the stair,
And by my bed he takes a chair,
And says in such a twinkly way,
"And how's the invalid to-day?"

He sees my tongue, he sees my throat;
He has a thing inside his coat
With which he listens at my chest;
And that is what I like the best.

He often makes me stay in bed,
When I would rather play instead,
And gives me horrid things to take,
In bottles that you have to shake.

And yet I really never mind,
Because he is so very kind.

Rose Fyleman

A Strange Baby

There was once a poor tabby cat whose kittens had died. She was very sad and lonely. The master of the house felt very sorry for her. Next day he went to a nearby wood and brought home a baby squirrel. This baby squirrel had lost his mother.

The master of the house had two children who were called Harry and Betty. They were twins and were seven years of age. Harry put the little creature in the box beside the cat. Then he and Betty watched to see what would happen.

At once the mother cat began to lick the baby squirrel. The little animal was so young that his eyes were not yet open. He could not even eat or drink by himself. Then pussy cat began to feed him just as if he was her own baby.

Mother cat took great care of baby squirrel. She nursed him and kept him warm at night. If a dog came near the box, she would get very angry. She would rush at the dog and chase him away.

When the squirrel grew bigger, many strange things began to happen. Mother cat did not know what to do. Her little son had a great big bushy tail. He did not walk in the same way as she did. He hopped about from place to place. Sometimes he would sit up on his hind legs.

That was not all.

They did not speak in the same kind of words. When the cat would say "miau", the squirrel would say "mir-mir."

Pussy showed him how to catch mice. He would turn away and not even bother to look at them. Poor pussy did her best, but it was of no use.

One day the cat and the squirrel went into the garden. At once the squirrel shot up the nearest tree. In a moment he was at the very top.

"Goodness!" said the cat in surprise. She was afraid that her son would hurt himself. "Come down at once!" she cried.

The squirrel did not come down. Instead, he began to show off. He darted from branch to branch very quickly. Pussy was sure that he would fall. Then he began to throw nuts at his cat mother. At last poor pussy left him and went back to the house.

The two animals lived very happily together. At night they slept beside each other in the same box. Sometimes the squirrel's bushy tail would rub against the cat's nose. Pussy would say "Stop tickling me!" Squirrel would then turn and say, "Give me more room!" Soon after, the two strange friends would be sound asleep.

Do You Remember ?

1. What was the name of the story?
2. Why was the tabby cat so sad?
3. What did the master of the house do?
4. What were the names of the twins?
5. Where did Harry put the little creature?
6. How did the cat take care of the squirrel?
7. What happened if a dog came near the box?
8. How was the squirrel different from the cat?
9. What did squirrel do when he went into the garden?
10. What did mother cat say to him?
11. Why did pussy leave the garden?
12. Where did they sleep at night?

Can You Tell ?

1. What names are given to young:
   (a) cats,   (b) dogs,   (c) sheep,   (d) pigs,
   (e) rabbits, (f) goats,   (g) cows, (h) horses?
2. What names are given to young:
   (a) foxes,   (b) wolves, (c) lions,   (d) bears,
   (e) hens,   (f) birds,   (g) ducks, (h) geese?
3. Name two animals which go to sleep during the winter.

Parents and Young

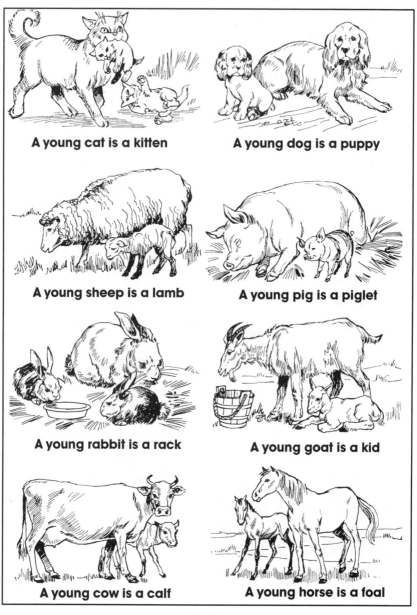

A young cat is a kitten

A young dog is a puppy

A young sheep is a lamb

A young pig is a piglet

A young rabbit is a rack

A young goat is a kid

A young cow is a calf

A young horse is a foal

Parents and Young

A young fox is a cub

A young wolf is a cub

A young lion is a cub

A young bear is a cub

A young hen is a chicken

A young bird is a nestling

A young duck is a duckling

A young goose is a gosling

Exercises

1. sheep, hen, cat, pig, goat, duck, horse, dog.
   (a) A kitten is a baby ____.
   (b) A puppy is a baby ____.
   (c) A lamb is a baby ____.
   (d) A piglet is a baby ____.
   (e) A chicken is a baby ____.
   (f) A duckling is a baby ____.
   (g) A foal is a baby ____.
   (h) A kid is a baby ____.

2. A **verb** is a **doing word**.
   Pick out the **doing words**.
   (a) The man walked quickly.
   (b) My sister wrote a letter.
   (c) On the table stood a lamp.
   (d) The girl lay where she fell.
   (e) She stopped and looked round.
   (f) The sun shone brightly.
   (g) The teacher spoke to the class.
   (h) Up the high pole climbed the monkey.
   (i) The boy came when I shouted.
   (j) He ran well and won a prize.

3. Choose the correct word in each bracket.

(a) He (would, wood) not chop the (would, wood).

(b) (Sum, some) boys were wrong in the (sum, some).

(c) I (knew, new) that she had bought a (knew, new) hat.

(d) No (one, won) could tell who had (one, won) the race.

(e) Last (week, weak) the child was ill and (week, weak).

Strange Talk

A little green frog lived under a log,
And every time he spoke,
Instead of saying, "Good-morning!"
He only said, "Croak! Croak!"

A duck lived by the water-side,
And little did she lack,
But when we asked, "How do you do?"
She only said, "Quack! Quack!"

A rook lived in an elm tree,
And all the world he saw,
But when he tried to make a speech,
It sounded like, "Caw! Caw!"

Three pups lived in a kennel,
And loved to make a row,
And when they meant, "May we go out?"
They said, "Bow-wow! Bow-wow!"

If all these creatures talked as much,
As little girls and boys,
And all of them tried to speak at once,
Wouldn't it make a noise?

Lucy E. Yates

The Bear and the Kettle

Once upon a time, a big brown bear lived in a large forest. It was winter, and the snow lay upon the ground. The bear was very hungry, because he could not find anything to eat.

At last, the animal left the woods to search for food. He went to a small village to see what he could get there. The bear reached the village without being seen. Quickly he ran to the back of the first house.

The door was open, and the hungry animal peeped in. He was very glad to see that there was nobody inside. The bear entered the kitchen, and began to sniff around. Alas! He could find no food to eat.

Suddenly the bear saw a kettle by the side of the fire. The water was boiling, and the steam was coming out of the spout. As the creature did not know what it was, he sniffed the steam. The bear gave a loud grunt of pain, because the steam burned his nose.

Now the bear had never felt anything like this before. He thought that the kettle was a strange kind of animal with a sting. The bear was very, very angry with this cheeky little creature.

"I'll teach you to sting my nose!" shouted the bear. He rushed at the kettle, and took it up in his paws. Then he crushed it against his breast. The more he squeezed it, the more he burnt himself.

This was too much for the bear. The big animal roared in pain and anger. He threw the kettle on the floor. Some of the boiling water fell on his feet, and hurt his toes. The bear began to jump madly about the room, because his feet were so sore.

130

Several people came to the house to find out the cause of all the noise. When the bear saw them, he knew that he was in danger. Some man would come with a gun and shoot him. He would need to escape at once.

With a grunt of rage, the bear rushed past the people at the door. He ran, and hopped, and jumped as fast as he could with his sore feet. The animal was very glad to reach the shelter of the forest.

Never again did the bear come near the village. He did not wish to meet the strange little creature with the terrible sting.

You and I know what really happened. The silly creature had tried to hurt the kettle, and had only hurt himself. All wise boys and girls know that they should not touch or go near a kettle of boiling water. It is very dangerous, because it can spill and burn you.

Do You Remember ?

1. Where did the bear live?
2. What colour was he?
3. Which season of the year was it?
4. Why was the animal so hungry?
5. Where did he go to find food?
6. What did the bear see beside the fire?
7. Why did the animal grunt in pain?
8. What did the bear think about the kettle?
9. What happened when he threw the kettle on the floor?
10. Why did the bear run back to the forest?
11. Why did he never again come to the village?
12. What should all wise boys and girls do?

Can You Tell ?

1. Name all the things you see on the next page of pictures.
2. What would you use to:
   (1) cut bread?   (2) boil water?
   (3) pour milk?   (4) sweep the floor?
   (5) lift the dirt?

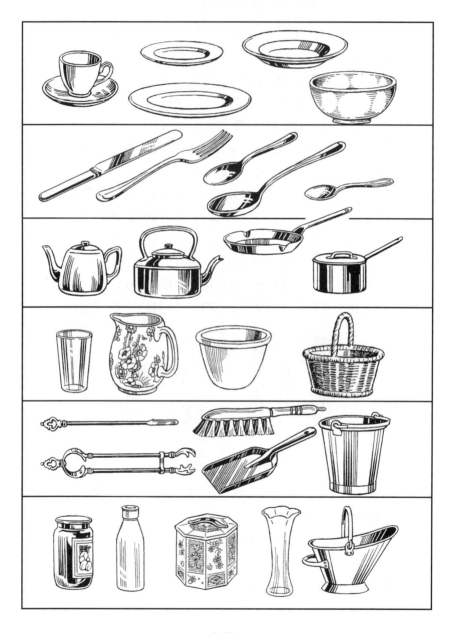

Exercises

1. money, milk, jam, water, books, dishes, flowers, sugar.
    (a) The kettle was full of ____.
    (b) The purse was full of ____.
    (c) The shelf was full of ____.
    (d) The jug was full of ____.
    (e) The bowl was full of ____.
    (f) The cupboard was full of ____.
    (g) The vase was full of ____.
    (h) The jar was full of ____.

2. Pick out the **verbs**.
    (a) The baby cried loudly.
    (b) The bird flew to her nest.
    (c) The cat sat beside the warm fire.
    (d) He asked me why I went.
    (e) Come and stand here.

3. cooker, table, floor, wall, chair, window, shelf.
    (a) The picture was on the ____.
    (b) The pot was on the ____.
    (c) The carpet was on the ____.
    (d) The cup was on the ____.
    (e) The clock was on the ____.
    (f) The curtain was on the ____.
    (g) The cushion was on the ____.

My Dog, Spot

I have a white dog,
Whose name is Spot,
And he's sometimes white,
And he's sometimes not.
But whether he's white
Or whether he's not,
There's a patch on his ear
That makes him Spot.

He has a tongue
That is long and pink
And he lolls it out
When he wants to think.
He seems to think most
When the weather is hot,
He's a wise sort of dog,
Is my dog, Spot.

He likes a bone
And he likes a ball,
But he doesn't care
For a cat at all.
He waggles his tail,
And he knows what's what,
So I'm glad that he's my dog,
My dog, Spot.

Rodney Bennett

The Farm

Many years ago when they were young, Dick and his sister Nan went to spend a week at their uncle's farm. Uncle Fred met them at the station and took them by car to his home. There they met Aunt Nell who had a nice tea ready for them. As they were very tired after their long journey, they went to bed early.

Next day started one of the most wonderful holidays they ever had. Dick went to work in the fields with his uncle. Nan helped her aunt with the jobs around the house. They were always busy as they had so many different things to do.

All too soon, the holiday came to an end, and Dick and Nan were very sorry to leave. They waved good-bye to their many animal friends and set off on the return journey. When they reached home they told their parents of the grand holiday they had spent at the farm. Here are the stories they told to their father and mother.

Nan's Story

I got up at seven o'clock every morning and helped Aunt Nell to make the breakfast. After breakfast, I washed the dishes and helped to tidy the house. It was my job to look after the chickens. I fed them with a mixture of meal, seed, and crumbs of bread. Afterwards I went to the coop and collected the eggs in a basket. Another of my jobs was to feed the little piglets. Their food was made up of all the scraps which had been left over from our meals. Next I went with Aunt Nell to watch her milk the cows.

Several times I tried to milk Daisy, the old brown cow, but I was not very good at it.

After dinner, I went to help Uncle Fred with his work in the fields. I raked the hay into small piles so that it could be easily gathered. When the cart was full, we had a jolly ride home on top of the hay.

After supper, I again visited and fed all my young farm friends. Every evening round the fireside, Uncle Fred told us wonderful tales of long ago. I always went to bed very tired but very happy.

Dick's Story

I did not get up as early as Nan, and had always to hurry to be in time for breakfast. Every morning I went with Uncle Fred to see if the sheep and lambs were safe and well. On our way back, we visited the fields to see how the crops were growing. There were fields of hay, wheat, potatoes, cabbages, and turnips.

One day the sheep were gathered together and driven into a pen by Betty, the clever collie. They were afterwards taken out one by one and sheared by Uncle Fred and a shepherd named Sam. This work is done in summer so that the sheep will not feel the cold when their coats of wool are cut off.

Another day we went to gather in the hay. I threw little bales of cut dry grass up on the cart. I did this with a hay-fork. We had a lovely picnic lunch in the field that day. After we had stored the hay in a shed, I had a ride on the back of old Tom, the farm horse.

After supper, Uncle Fred and I went to see if everything was all right in the stable, the byre, and the pig-sty. Before going to bed, Uncle Fred would tell us stories of great heroes of olden days. He was so interesting that I could listen to him all night.

Do You Remember ?

1. What was the name of the story?
2. How long did Dick and Nan spend at the farm?
3. Where did Uncle Fred meet them?
4. Who had tea ready for them?
5. When did Nan rise every morning?
6. How did she help Aunt Nell?
7. What food did she give to
   (a) the chickens, (b) the piglets?
8. Where did Dick go every morning?
9. Who gathered the sheep for shearing?
10. Why is this work done in summer?
11. How did Dick help in the hay field?
12. What did Uncle Fred tell them round the fireside?

Can You Tell ?

1. What is a farm?
2. Why does a farmer keep
   (a) cows, (b) hens, (c) sheep, (d) pigs?
3. What kinds of food do these creatures eat?
4. How often does a farmer milk the cows?
5. What is made from milk?
6. Why does a farmer plough his fields?
7. What is grown on a farm?
8. Of what use is a scarecrow?
9. Which creature wakens the others?
10. What is a (a) stable, (b) sty, (c) coop, (d) barn?

What the farm animals give us

Hen	**Eggs** **Meat** **Feathers for pillow**
Sheep	**Mutton** **Woollen scarves** **Rugs** **Carpets**
Pig	**Bacon** **Ham** **Leather** **Lard** BEST LARD
Cow	**Butter** **Beef** Milk **Milk** **Cheese** **Leather**
Horse	**Chair covers** **Hair stuffing** **Glue**
Goat	**Milk** **Shawl** **Gloves** **Wool**

The Story of Wheat

The farmer sowed the seed

Spraying killed the weeds

The wheat grew

The farmer threshed it

The miller ground it

The baker baked it

Mother bought it

We eat it as bread

Exercises

1. leather, wool, paper, wood, glass, silk, rubber steel, china, silver.
   (a) A table is made of ____.
   (b) A window is made of ____.
   (c) A book is made of ____.
   (d) A shoe is made of ____.
   (e) A jersey is made of ____.
   (f) A ring is made of ____.
   (g) A ball is made of ____.
   (h) A knife is made of ____.
   (i) A ribbon is made of ____.
   (j) A cup is made of ____.

2. Give words **opposite in meaning** to:
   (a) shallow,   (b) pretty,
   (c) early,   (d) inside,
   (e) start,   (f) front.

3. (a) Pick out **nouns**.
       (1) The price of the book was five dollars.
       (2) The mouse pulled the cheese into the hole.
       (3) Father and Jane went to Liverpool by train.
   (b) Pick out **verbs**.
       (1) The ball broke the window.
       (2) I told him how I knew.
       (3) Run away and play.

4. Choose the correct word in each bracket.

(a) She told a (tale, tail) about a cat's (tale, tail).

(b) He will (right, write) to say that you are (right, write).

(c) (Our, Hour) train leaves in an (our, hour).

(d) (To, Two) men went (to, two) the market.

(e) (Their, There) books are lying over (their, there).

"I," said the duck. "I call it fun,
For I have my pretty red rubbers on;
They make a little three-toed track,
In the soft, cool mud — quack! quack!"

"I," cried the dandelion. "I,
My roots are thirsty, my buds are dry,"
And she lifted up her yellow head,
Out of her green and grassy bed.

Sang the brook, "I welcome every drop,
Come down, dear raindrops, never stop,
Until a broad river you make of me,
And then I will carry you to the sea."

"I," shouted Ted, "for I can run,
With my high top-boots and raincoat on,
Through every puddle and stream and
    pool,
I find on the road to school."

Anonymous

The Cat and the Goldfish

"Inky! You naughty pussy! Go away at once!" cried Jim. He chased the big black cat out of the room.

"What was he doing?" asked his sister, Alice.

"I found him on the table at the window," said Jim. "He was trying to catch the goldfish. He was about to put his paw into the bowl."

"Oh dear!" said his sister. "We will need to keep him out of this room. He will eat our two little goldfish."

"I've got a clever idea," replied Jim. "I'm going to teach Inky a lesson."

The boy took the bowl of goldfish away. He put the two little fish into a basin of water.

"Don't worry!" he said to the goldfish. "You will soon be back again in your own little bowl."

"What are you going to do?" asked his sister.

"Just wait and see!" replied Jim. "Go and bring the little toy fish. You will find them in the big toy box."

Alice soon returned with two little toy fish in her hand. Her brother took them and put them into the glass bowl. He then filled the bowl with water from the tap.

"Now we will teach Mr. Inky a lesson!" he said.

Jim and Alice returned to the room. The boy placed the bowl with the toy fish on the table. Then they hid behind a big chair to watch the fun. They had not long to wait.

Inky came slowly and quietly into the room. He thought that no one was there. With a quick jump he was up on the table.

"What a treat!" he purred to himself. "Now I can catch two nice little fish for my dinner."

Jim and Alice saw the cat put his paw into the bowl. He scooped out one of the little toy fish. Crunch! Inky bit it in two. He tried to swallow a part but it nearly choked him. What a horrible taste it had!

"That one must be bad," said Inky. "I'll try the other one."

The cat scooped the other fish out of the bowl. He tried to eat it but soon dropped it. This fish tasted much worse than the first one.

"Strange!" said Inky to himself. "I like fish. These goldfish have a horrible taste. I will never try to catch or eat a goldfish again." Inky walked out of the room in disgust.

When the cat had gone, Jim and Alice came out of hiding. They laughed and joked about poor Inky. Jim took away the bowl and the broken toy fish. He returned soon afterwards with the real goldfish in the bowl.

It is funny to watch Inky. He comes into the room as usual. He looks at the bowl of goldfish in disgust. He never goes near it. "Pooh!" he says to himself. "Goldfish have a horrible taste."

Do You Remember ?

1. What was the name of the story?
2. Why was the cat called Inky?
3. Why did Jim chase pussy out of the room?
4. Where were the goldfish?
5. How many were there?
6. What did Jim do with them?
7. What did he put in their place?
8. Where did Alice get the toy fish?
9. How did Inky catch the fish?
10. What happened when he tried to eat them?
11. What did the cat do?
12. Why does Inky never go near the goldfish?

Can You Tell ?

1. How does a cat show that it is happy?
2. How does a cat show that it is angry?
3. What does a cat like to eat?
4. What should a cat wear round its neck? Tell why.
5. Which creatures do cats chase?
6. Give some pet names of cats.
7. How is a cat able to walk so quietly?
8. Name some kinds of big wild cats.

Cats

Common cat   Persian   Siamese   Manx

Lion   Tiger   Leopard   Black Panther

Exercises

1. *(a)* A cat is (a bird, an animal, a fish).
   (b) A cat has (two, four, six) legs.
   (c) A cat has a coat of (wool, feathers, fur).
   (d) A cat (mews, barks, crows).
   (e) A cat's foot is called a (hoof, horn, paw).
   (f) A baby cat is called a (puppy, kitten, calf).
   (g) A cat is fond of (cold, heat, ice).
2. We use **was** when we speak of **one**.
   We use **were** when we speak of **more than one**.
   Put **was** or **were** in the spaces.
   (a) The book __ lost.   *(b)* The boys __ hungry.
   (c) The dishes __ broken.
   (d) The place __ dark.
   (e) She __ happy.   *(f)* They __ glad.
3. Give the **plural** of: *(a)* wall, *(b)* match,
   (c) puppy, *(d)* calf, *(e)* goose.
4. Choose the correct word in each bracket.
   (a) We could not (sea, see) the (sea, see).
   (b) The boy (threw, through) a stone (threw, through) the window.
   (c) I (herd, heard) the lowing of the (herd, heard) of cattle.
   (d) The brown (bear, bare) chased the American Indian who had (bear, bare) feet.
   (e) The man (blue, blew) till he was almost (blue, blew) in the face.

Anansi in Trinidad

Anansi, the clever spider, left a letter for his mother and father. In it he said that he was going to go to America and he would write to them from there. He did not go to America for he crept aboard the wrong jet and was unloaded at Trinidad along with a basket of yams in which he was sleeping. The yams were taken off the jet and put on the bus to San Fernando. They were delivered to Jean Khan at St. Joseph's Village.

Robin or Anansi as he now called himself made his home in the basement of Jean Khan's house and was soon causing very strange things to happen. Each night when the maid went out to collect the dry washing she would find something missing or she might find something on the drying line which didn't belong to them but belonged to Mrs. Smith next door.

Anansi would sometimes take a handkerchief down the hill to the market and would sell it to one of his friends for food, saying that he had just bought it. Then he would tell the policeman that Mrs. Cat or Mr. Rat or Miss Blackbird had a handkerchief belonging to Jean Khan. He would watch from the top of the tree. How he would laugh when the police came to take away Mrs. Cat, Mr. Rat or Miss Blackbird and return the hanky.

Soon his tricks got him into great trouble with all the other animals and he had to leave San Fernando.

The Elves
and the Shoemaker

Long, long ago, there lived a shoemaker and his wife. They were honest and hard-working. They were also kind to those who needed help.

Times were hard and work was very scarce. The shoemaker became poorer and poorer until he had no food and no money. All he had left was just enough leather to make one pair of shoes.

One evening, the shoemaker cut out the shoes, all ready to make the next day. He left the pieces of leather on the table. Tired and weary, he went to bed.

In the morning, the shoemaker rose early to start work on the shoes. To his great surprise, he found they were already made and standing side by side on the table. He picked them up and looked at them very carefully. They were so well done that he could not find one single bad stitch in them.

That same morning a man came in to buy a pair of shoes. When he saw how well they were made, he paid the shoemaker a good price. The shoemaker was now able to buy leather for two pairs. Again he cut them out in the evening, meaning to rise early the next day to finish them.

There was no need, for in the morning two lovely pairs of shoes stood on the table.

These shoes were soon sold and the shoemaker bought leather for four pairs. He cut them out at night and laid out the pieces as before. When he came down in the morning, the shoes were finished and ready for sale.

This went on day after day. So good was his trade that the shoemaker soon became very rich.

One evening just before Christmas, he said to his wife, "My dear, I would like to find out who is helping us. Let us sit up tonight and watch."

That evening, they hid themselves in a corner of the workshop. At midnight, two little brownies came running into the room. They climbed up on the table and took up the pieces of leather. Then they began to stitch and sew and hammer.

They worked so well and so fast that, in a short time, all the shoes were done. As soon as they were finished, they jumped off the table and ran away.

Next morning, the shoemaker said to his wife, "Those little brownies have been very kind to us. What can we do to show our thanks?"

"I have a good idea," said his wife. "It is very cold and I will make them warm clothes. You can make them nice little shoes."

When everything was ready, the shoemaker and his wife laid the clothes and the shoes on the table. Then they hid to see what the little brownies would do. At midnight they came running into the room, ready to begin work. Instead of pieces of leather, they saw the pretty little clothes and shoes. They shouted with joy and put them on. Soon after they left singing and dancing.

Everything went well with the kind shoemaker and his wife. They were rich and happy for the rest of their lives.

Do You Remember ?

1. What was the name of the story?
2. What kind of people were the shoemaker and his wife?
3. Why did the shoemaker become very poor?
4. What was all he had left?
5. What did he do before going to bed?
6. What did he find in the morning?
7. What did he do on the next evening?
8. What did he find on the following morning?
9. What did the shoemaker say to his wife?
10. What did they see when they sat up to watch?
11. How did they show their thanks?
12. What happened to the kind shoemaker and his wife?

Can You Tell ?

1. A **shoemaker** is a man who makes and mends shoes.
   Give a sentence about each of the following:
   (a) a chimney sweep,   (b) a house painter,
   (c) a gardener,   (d) a joiner,
   (e) a plumber,   (f) a baker,
   (g) a butcher,   (h) a grocer.
2. A **shop assistant** is a person who sells things in a shop. Give a sentence about each of the following:
   (a) a waitress,   (b) a hairdresser,
   (c) a florist,   (d) a chemist,
   (e) a cook,   (f) a dressmaker,
   (g) a nanny,   (h) a typist.

Occupations

Painter

Doctor

Chef

Engineer

Plumber

Grocer

Joiner

Teacher

Occupations

Florist

Scientist

Gardener

Nanny

Waitress

Hairdresser (Lady)

Secretary

Shop Assistant

Exercises

1. sheep, coal, letters, pictures, luggage, suits.
    (a) A postman brings ____ .
    (b) A shepherd watches ____ .
    (c) An artist paints ____ .
    (d) A miner digs for ____ .
    (e) A tailor makes ____ .
    (f) A porter carries ____ .

2. Put **was** or **were** in the spaces.
    (a) ____ the dresses pretty?
    (b) ____ the stone heavy?
    (c) ____ he in good time?
    (d) ____ we first?
    (e) They ____ frightened but I ____ not.
    (f) The spelling ____ easy but the sums ____
        difficult.

3. Which of these would you like to be?
    silly, stupid, good, cruel, happy, kind, lazy,
    clever, tidy, selfish, wise.

4. "Excuse me!" "Thank you!" "Hush!" "Good-
    bye!" "Oh!" "Hullo!"

    Which do I say when I:
    (a) get something?   (b) meet a friend?
    (c) go in front?   (d) am surprised?
    (e) want quietness?   (f) leave a friend?

A clear little spring bubbled up from a hill,
And grew to a brook before long,
It ran through a farmyard, and flowing on
   still,
Began to grow deeper and strong,
And then came a village and nearby a mill,
And a ferryman rowing his boat;
Some little brown rabbits who lived in a
   hill,
And a donkey, a dog and a goat.
And now it's grown into a river at last,
As it flows along shining and free;
There are tugs and some barges and ships
   sailing fast,
For the river has come to the sea.

Anonymous

Once there was an old man who lived alone in a little hut. He worked at odd jobs for the people who lived near him. Everyone liked him because he was so kind and happy.

One day the old man was sitting on the doorstep of his little home. He was eating a big red apple and enjoying the warm sunshine. As he sat there he thought and thought and thought.

"What can I do to make others happy?" he asked himself. "I am old and not very clever. There must be some way in which I can help people."

All at once, a smile came over his face. "I know what I will do," he said. "Why did I not think of it before?"

Then a very strange thing happened.

Everywhere he worked, the old man asked for part of his pay in apples. He took the apples home and ate them. He saved all the cores and put them into a bag.

The people of the village thought that he was strange. Some said that he was crazy. The boys and girls did not believe this.

"He is not crazy," they said. "He is a wise old man and we are very fond of him. We know that he puts all his apple-cores into a bag. That is why we call him Old Apple-seed John."

One day Old John locked the door of his little home and tramped away. In one hand he had a walking stick. On his back he carried a big bag of apple-cores.

Old Apple-seed John walked far into the country. Now and again he stopped by the side of the road. The old man made a hole in the ground with his stick. Then he dropped an apple-core into the hole and covered it with earth.

All summer he wandered from place to place. Everywhere he went, Old Apple-seed John planted his cores by the sides of the roads. When his bag was empty, he went back to work. Always he asked for part of his pay in apples.

When his bag was full of apple-cores, Old John would set off again. Sometimes a farmer would say to him, "Stay here. I will give you a good job and pay you well." The old man would shake his head and say,

"Old Apple-seed John has work to do,
And he must go on to carry it through,
To plant seeds here, to plant seeds there, And so have apple-trees everywhere."

In this way the kind old man spent the rest of his life. Fine trees grew from the cores which he planted. Every autumn they were covered with apples.

Passers-by often stopped to eat some of the fruit. "How nice it is to see such lovely apple trees," they said. "Who planted them here?"

The people who lived in those parts knew the answer. They told the strangers the wonderful story of Old Apple-seed John.

Do You Remember ?

1. What was the name of the story?
2. What strange thing did the old man do?
3. What did the village people think? Explain.
4. What did the boys and girls say?
5. When did Old John set off?
6. What did he have in his hand?
7. What did he carry on his back?
8. How did he plant the apple-cores?
9. How did Old Apple-seed John earn his living?
10. What did some farmers ask him to do?
11. What answer did the old man give?
12. In which season were the trees covered with apples?

Can You Tell ?

1. Name as many different kinds of fruit as you can.
2. Which fruits are big and which fruits are very small?
3. Which fruits should be eaten without the skins?
4. Which fruit do you like best? Tell why.
5. Which fruits grow only in very hot countries?

Further Activity

Collect some seeds from different fruits. Plant them in the classroom. Watch them grow. Measure them. Keep a graph of the different seeds. Draw them as they grow. Describe them.

Fruit

Apple

Orange

Plum

Banana

Melon

Lemon

Cherries

Peach

Gooseberry

Strawberry

Grapes

Pear

Pineapple

Coconut

Raspberry

Exercises

1. yellow, red, green, orange, brown.
    What colours are these fruits when ripe?
    pears, bananas, limes, strawberries, oranges.

2. Give the **opposites** of:
    (a) The **night** was **cold** and **wet**.
    (b) The **giant** was **tall** and **fat**.
    (c) The **question** was **long** and **difficult**.

3. Put **there is** or **there are** in the spaces.
    (a) __ __ a big pond on the farm.
    (b) On the desk __ __ some papers.
    (c) Near the road __ __ a forest.
    (d) __ __ seven days in a week.

4. You should be able to answer these questions.
    (a) What is your full name ?
    (b) Where do you stay ?
    (c) How old are you ?
    (d) When is your birthday ?
    (e) What colour are your eyes ?
    (f) What is your telephone number ?
    (g) How many brothers have you ? Name them.
    (h) How many sisters have you ? Name them.
    (i) Which school do you attend ?
    (j) Where would you like to go on holiday ? Tell why.

My Shadow

I have a little shadow that goes in and out
    with me,
And what can be the use of him is more than
    I can see.
He is very, very like me, from the heels
    up to the head;
And I see him jump before me, when I
    jump into my bed.

The funniest thing about him is the way
    he likes to grow,
Not at all like proper children which is
    always very slow;
For he sometimes shoots up taller like
    an India-rubber ball,
And he sometimes gets so little that there's
    none of him at all.

He hasn't got a notion of how children
    ought to play,
And can only make a fool of me in every
    sort of way.
He stays so close beside me, he's a coward
    you can see;
I'd think shame to stick to nanny as that
    shadow sticks to me.

One morning, very early, before the sun
    was up,
I rose and found the shining dew on every
    buttercup;
But my lazy little shadow, like an arrant
    sleepy-head,
Had stayed at home behind me and was
    fast asleep in bed.

R.L. Stevenson

Boom-Boom !

A boy lay ill in hospital. His name was Frank and he was seven years of age. The doctor was very worried because he would not take any food.

His mother and father sat beside the bed and looked sadly down at him. Frank lay quite still and stared at the wall in front of him. He took no interest in anything and seldom spoke. His parents brought him all kinds of toys but Frank did not bother to play with them.

"Is there anything you want?" asked his father.

"No, I don't want anything!" replied Frank.

His mother bent down and whispered in his ear as if it was a great secret. "Tell me what you want," she said. "Mother will get it for you. "

Suddenly Frank stretched out his hand and cried, "I want to see Boom-Boom! I want to see Boom-Boom!"

His poor mother did not know what to say. She looked at her husband in surprise. Who was Boom-Boom?

Father gave a little smile when he heard the name. He remembered it well. He and Frank had been to the circus shortly before his illness. The funny clown was called Boom-Boom. Every time he told them his name, the big drums made a loud boom-boom.

That same evening the father came back to the hospital with a toy clown under his arm. Frank just looked at it and said, "That is not Boom-Boom! I want to see Boom-Boom!"

Next day Frank was still very ill. His father wished that he could wrap him up in his blankets and take him to the circus. Then he said to himself, "Frank cannot go to see Boom-Boom. I wonder if Boom-Boom can come to see Frank?"

The father went to the circus but the show was closed. He then went to the clown's home and told him about Frank. Mr. Moreno, which was the real name of the clown, said that he would help him.

"He wants to see me, does he? I will go with you at once."

When they reached the hospital room, the father opened the door and shouted, "Look, Frank! Here is Boom-Boom!"

Frank sat up in bed and looked at the well-dressed man who was with his father. "No, no!" he cried. "He is not Boom-Boom!"

"The boy is quite right," said the man. "I am not Boom-Boom. I am Mr. Moreno." With a smile, he turned and left the room. An hour later the door opened and in came the funniest clown in the world. His face was chalk-white with large black spots on his nose and cheeks. He wore a clown's hat and a dress of every colour of the rainbow.

Frank sat up in bed and shouted with joy. "Hullo, Boom-Boom! I am so glad to see you!" The clown performed some of his jumping tricks and the boy clapped his hands in glee.

When the doctor came to visit Frank, he was surprised to see a clown sitting at the bedside. The funny man was giving the boy a glass of hot milk and saying, "Drink this, and Boom-Boom will come back to see you tomorrow."

Frank drank the milk. "Is it good?" asked Boom-Boom.

"Yes, Boom-Boom! It is very good!"

The clown turned to the doctor. "Doctor," he said. "You must not be jealous. My jokes are much better than your medicine."

The doctor laughed and replied, "So it seems!"

From that day onwards, till Frank was better, Boom-Boom came to the hospital every afternoon. In two weeks the boy was ready to go home.

"What do I owe you, Boom-Boom?" asked the father. "I must pay you for all your trouble."

"You owe me nothing," said the clown. "I am very glad that I was able to help you." With a smile he turned to the boy and said, "Good-bye Frank! You are better now. I think I will put on my visiting card . . . Boom-Boom, Circus-Clown and Assistant Doctor."

Jules Claretie (Adapted)

Do You Remember ?

1. What was the name of the story?
2. Where was the boy?
3. What was his name?
4. Why was the doctor worried?
5. Who was Boom-Boom?
6. What did Frank's father do?
7. What was the clown's real name?
8. What happened on his first visit?
9. How was he dressed on his second visit?
10. What had Frank to take?
11. What did the clown say to the doctor?
12. What was he going to put on his visiting card?

Can You Tell ?

1. What shape is a circus?
2. What is the name of the large tent?
3. What is (1) a ringmaster, (2) a clown, (3) an acrobat?
4. Name animals which perform in the circus.
5. What do you see in each of the circus pictures? Write a short story.
6. *(a)* Where do circus people live?
   (b) Why do they live in them?

The Circus

Exercises

1. Write correctly:
   - *(a)* there are thirty days in april
   - *(b)* my brother james is going to london
   - *(c)* we saw miss smith on friday
2. What is a:
   - *(a)* miner, butcher, barber, shoemaker, waiter?
   - *(b)* sailor, doctor, tailor, pilot, soldier?
3. Give the **plural** of:
   > key, hero, daisy, half, ox.
4. Give words **opposite in meaning** to:
   > rich, clean, new, asleep, first.
5. Which letter is silent in each of these words:
   > wrong, lamb, knob, calm, honest?
6. Name an animal, a bird, a flower, and a fruit beginning with the letter B. Do the same with the letters C and P and S.

45   **Choosing Shoes**

New shoes, new shoes,
Red and pink and blue shoes,
Tell me, what would **you** choose,
    If they'd let us buy?

Buckle-shoes, bow shoes,
Pretty pointy-toe shoes,
Strappy, cappy low shoes,
    Let's have some to try.

Bright shoes, white shoes,
Dandy-dance-by-night shoes —
Perhaps-a-little-tight shoes,
    Like some? so would I.

but

Flat shoes, fat shoes,
Stump-along-like-that shoes,
Wipe-them-on-the-mat shoes,
— That's the sort they'll buy.

ffrida Wolfe

Danger by the Seaside 46

When you wade, don't go too deep
close to the shore it's best to keep.

Don't climb fences, rocks or walls,
or you may have some nasty falls.

From the cliff edge keep away,
it's wiser on the path to stay.

Caves are dangerous when the tide
is coming in, so stay outside!

When walking on a quay or pier,
watch the edge, don't go too near.

Don't stand up when in a boat,
sit quite still when you're afloat.

Your Dictionary

Write out any new words you have learnt and give their meanings.

_____

_____

_____

_____

_____

_____

_____

_____

_____

_____

_____

_____

_____

_____

_____

_____

_____

_____

_____

Printed by Bell & Bain Ltd., Glasgow, U.K.